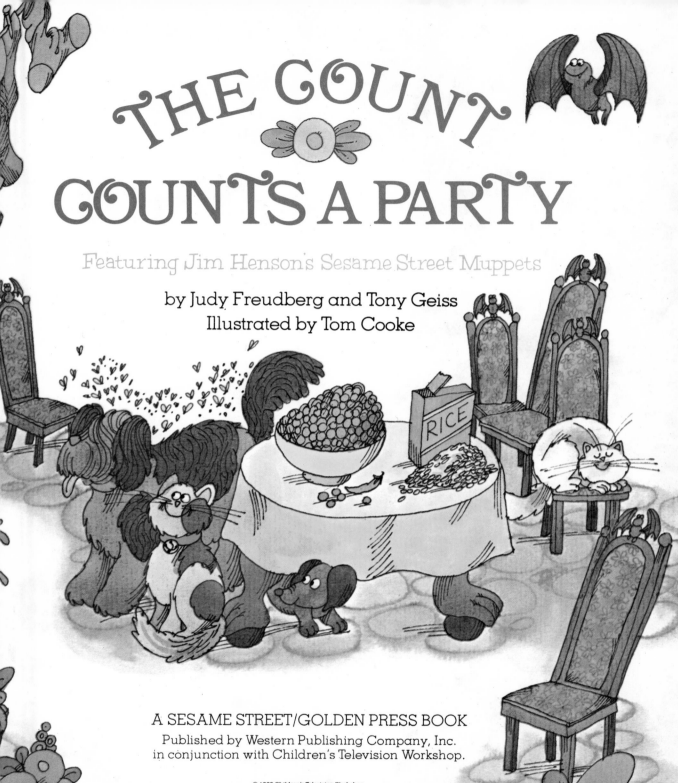

THE COUNT
COUNTS A PARTY

Featuring Jim Henson's Sesame Street Muppets

by Judy Freudberg and Tony Geiss
Illustrated by Tom Cooke

A SESAME STREET/GOLDEN PRESS BOOK
Published by Western Publishing Company, Inc.
in conjunction with Children's Television Workshop.

© 1980 Children's Television Workshop.
The Count and other Muppet characters © 1980 Muppets, Inc. All rights reserved. Printed in U.S.A.
SESAME STREET®, the SESAME STREET SIGN, and THE SESAME STREET BOOK CLUB are trademarks and service marks of
Children's Television Workshop
GOLDEN® and GOLDEN PRESS® are trademarks of Western Publishing Company, Inc.
No part of this book may be reproduced or copied in any form without written permission from the publisher
Library of Congress Catalog Card Number: 79-92157
ISBN 0-307-23106-2

One day the Count sat in his castle amidst all the things he liked to count, and he was very sad.

"Woe is me," he said. "I cannot think of anything new to count. I have counted everything! I have counted:

Dogs and cats,
Frogs and bats,
Plants and rocks,
Pants and socks.

Fleas and mice,
Peas and rice,
Chairs and clouds,
Hairs and crowds.
I've counted big,
I've counted small.
There's nothing left to count at all!"

He sobbed.
"One sob," said the Count.
And he sighed.
"One sigh," said the Count, "and
one teardrop! Alas, what is there
left for me to count?"

RICE

He thought of everything he could possibly count, beginning with the letter A and going through the alphabet.

"Aardvarks I have counted, ants I have counted," he said. "Apples I have counted...." He went on until he reached the letter P. "Parades I have counted, parasols I have counted, parrots I have counted, parties...*I have not counted!*"

"That's it! *Parties!*" shouted the Count, startling his
pet bats. "I have never counted parties. Eureka! I will
give a party for all my friends on Sesame Street... and I
will *count the party!*"

"Yay!" said the bats, fluttering about his head in
happy circles. "Party, party, party! We're going to have
a party!"

And the Count began to prepare for his party.

First he cleaned the castle from basement to belfry. He borrowed a broom from the witch next door and swept all the dust into a big pile, and then swept the big pile under a big rug.

"One sweep, two sweeps, three sweeps, four sweeps!" said the Count. "Ah-ah-ah!"

Then he took down all the dirty old cobwebs and hung up clean new cobwebs.

He even told his bats to take a bat-bath in their bat-tub.

"Lyuba," he said to his number-one bat, "don't forget to wash behind your wings. You, too, darlings."

"Don't worry," said the bats, "we'll get squeaky clean. Squeak, squeak, squeak!"

"Now," said the Count, "I will have nineteen friends from Sesame Street at my party. That makes twenty friends, counting me. (And I *love* to count me!) So I will need twenty plates. Ah-ah-ah! And twenty party balloons! Ah-ah-ah! And a party hat for everyone! Twenty party hats! Ah-ah-ah-ah!"

"And what else?" asked the Count. "I know!
Something to eat!"

First, he baked a chocolate layer cake, and then he
counted the twenty lovely layers.

"Nobody should eat just cake," said the Count, "so we'll have some fruit! Twenty apples. Twenty! And twenty peaches. Twenty! And for the big eaters ...twenty watermelons!"

Then he set the table with twenty plates, and it was time for the party to begin!

The Count let down the drawbridge. On the front path to his castle he laid out twenty welcome mats. Then he waited for his friends.

He waited... and waited... and waited... and waited. Nobody came!

"Woe is me!" said the Count. "I have waited twenty minutes and nobody has come to my party. What have I done wrong?"

"Woe is us, too!" said his bats. "No party, no party, no party!"

"Wait!" said the Count, "I know why nobody has come. I forgot to invite them!"

And, like a flash of his own lightning, he sat down and wrote twenty invitations (one for himself, too) saying, "Stop everything and come right away—1,2,3—to my castle for a party. Come as you are. Do not even change your clothes. Hurry, hurry, hurry! Signed, Your Friendly Local Count."

He gave the invitations to his bats, who flew off to deliver the invitations to Sesame Street.

When Ernie and Bert got their invitations, Ernie was
in the bathtub and Bert was waiting to take his bath.
They started right out to the Count's castle.

Cookie Monster was eating a box of delicious cookies when he got his invitation. He ate the invitation, too, and then dashed off to the party.

Oscar got his invitation and ran toward the castle as fast as he could. He planned to tell the Count, "I don't want to come to your rotten party!"

When the Amazing Mumford got his invitation, he was pulling rabbits out of his hat. So when he set off for the party, he was followed by a trail of rabbits.

Big Bird was playing hopscotch, so he *hopped* all the way to the party.

Super-Grover was flying around looking for someone in distress when Lyuba delivered the invitation. He sped to the castle with his cape streaming behind him, and landed in the moat.

Twenty minutes after he sent the invitations,
the Count looked out the castle door and saw the
whole gang coming up the path.

"Aha!" said the Count. "My friends are coming.
I knew I could count on them!"

"Yay!" said the bats, as they flew back into the
castle. "It's party time!"

"Wait! Not so fast, my pets," said the Count. "I must count everybody!"

So, while everyone waited patiently, the Count counted his guests.

"1,2,3,4,5,6,7,8,9,10,11,12,13,14,15,16,17, 18,19 . . . only 19? But there should be twenty. Who is missing? Oh, of course. I forgot to count myself! How silly of me! I, the Count, make twenty. Twenty playful party people! Ah-ah-ah-ah!"

"And twenty batty bats!" shrieked the bats. "Strike up the band!"

As the band played the Transylvania Polka twenty times, everybody danced and ate and danced some more and ate some more. The party lasted for twenty hours, and the Count was very, very happy.

"One! One *wonderful* party!" exclaimed the Count ecstatically. "Ah-ah-ah-ah-ah-ah!!!"

ABCDEFGHI